THE BEAST OF BLACKBURN LANE

A MODERN DAY HORROR STORY

LESLIE J CUNEO

Author's Acknowledgement

Ladies and Gentlemen, I, the author thank you for taking the time to read this story. What started as a few coincidences, morphed into a totally consuming nightmare. This is the attempt at documenting these events and setting my pen to paper.

I would like to take this opportunity to acknowledge and thank a few people.

First, to my brother in law Peter, the avid outdoorsman. Who hunts, fishes, kills and cooks anything that walks, runs, flies or swims. You have given me great suggestions. Thank you.

Next, to my Cousin Joe, whose property in Montauk inspired me. His house is on top of Prospect Hill and is adjacent to the "Hunting Grounds" and whose personal tours of Camp Hero and surrounding State Parks were invaluable. Thank you for allowing me to tap into your vast knowledge of the area.

Also, to my friend Steve, aka "Sarge" for providing me with research on Police tactics, aviation and military research and tactics. All things said about him were true. I wish to say, thank you and enjoy retirement from the department and good luck with your new career.

Lastly, to my family for their support during this time of my physical and mental challenges, writing this story.

Now, I would like you to get comfortable, perhaps sit back or lay down, dim the lights. You are about to be immersed in the horror I called,

The Beast of Blackburn Lane.

Leslie J Cuneo

Author/Survivor

CONTENTS

Chapter 1

The Beast of Blackburn Lane

So , for as long as I can remember I do not sleep. It is particularly bad on nights of a full moon when the moon is high over head. As a child, I remember pacing the house after midnight. Looking outside and seeing the full moon casting light all over the backyard.

As I grew older it only got worse.

My sister started to work for me. One day, I complained in my office how I had gotten very little sleep the night before. She said "silly, don't you know it was a full moon last night." She further stated "don't you know we don't sleep well under a full moon!" Actually, I thought, No, I did not know that.

Flash forward a few years. After my surgeries and amputations, I slept downstairs in a family room with a lot of windows. A bank of five foot high windows was in my room. Located about three feet off of the ground. It allowed me to see anything in my backyard. Here in lies the problem. It allowed anyone or anything to see me in my room from the backyard.

So, late one night, when the moon was full and bright, I noticed the usual night sounds were gone. No crickets, cicadas, no insects of any kind. If I were in a forest hunting, I would have said a predator was nearby. But I was in a small affluent New York suburb. Not exactly the habitat for a large alpha predator. That uneasy nervous feeling that someone or something was watching me started to creep over me. The hair on my body stood up and I felt very nauseous.

I was afraid to look. I wanted to see but yet again, I did not. A large dark shape was just out of my clear vision. It had not triggered the outdoor security lights. It seemed to know how to avoid them. That meant it was intelligent. Probably the neighbor's dog. I put it off to nerves, something I ate or a movie I had watched on Television. I decided to roll over, not look and try to sleep.

I dozed off for a respite, but was awakened by what seemed to be twigs snapping. As I rolled over and looked to the window. All I saw was a pair of glowing yellow eyes in the tree line. Again, as a hunter, it was not a normal eye shine you might see from deer or the like. These were glowing, piercing, fierce eyes. It looked like a dog. Maybe a German Shepard. It got closer but slowly. The lights had come on automatically, it did not flinch it just continued towards the windows. I was relieved to see it it looked like a very large dog. It had black fur with a tan under belly. It looked normal, that is to say until it got to the window and stood up on two legs and walked like a human.

It pressed it's face near the glass. And I nearly vomited because of what I saw. It was not a dog. Long face, terrible teeth, pointy ears on top of its head and those eyes. The terrible glowing eyes. Now I knew coyotes had been making a comeback all over the country. But this was no coyote, nor was it a wolf. This was half man, half wolf, it was a Beast! I was terrified. I had no way to defend myself, my guns were locked away. Only thing between me and it, was three panes of glass.

It seemed to feed off of my fear.

I now heard it breathing and snarling. As it's clawed hands came up it started to tap on the window to get my attention. At that point, it seemed I vomited and fainted. I awoke a few minutes later to find my visitor had vanished. I was just beside myself. Was it a dream? The vomit on the floor told me otherwise. As I looked at the window, I saw the claw marks and scratches that had come from it's tapping.

As a result, I have multiple security systems with cameras. Every door, every window is covered. Glass sensors, infrared and cameras. Was I crazy? Perhaps. I started to sleep during the day, and at night I kept an eye out for the Beast of Blackburn Lane…waiting for it's return.

Chapter 2

The Beast of Blackburn Lane Returns

Although I grew up in Port Washington, I was born and now live in Manhasset for over thirty five years. So, I was familiar with the natural animals in the area. Squirrels, rabbits, raccoons an occasional possum and one snow owl that was about the limitation of what I had seen. Rumors of deer, coyotes and foxes I had heard, but not seen.

So, I thought it was raccoons that always attacked the garbage cans on the side of the house. We bought tighter, bigger garbage cans and a garage to put them in. But it deflected nothing. I was surprised when the rabbits who were always in my yard in 2002, when we moved in, had all but disappeared. Lastly, my dogs suddenly barked at what appeared to be nothing in the backyard. They looked out the window and let out low growls not really barking. They seemed more afraid then anything else.

In the summer, when outside barbecuing at night, I had noticed that large amounts of food had gone missing, when left outside. Raw or cooked it did not matter. No squirrel or raccoon was taking a serving tray of meat. When it happened, that uneasy feeling would wash over me.

Later, that night I heard the tapping and scratching at the back door in the kitchen. It moved eight feet to the bay window in the kitchen.

Rapping and tapping. My house was brick so I only heard it on the window frames and glass. A few minutes later it moved ten feet to the window directly in front of my bed. All my windows were side by side twelve inch wide casement windows. This one was five feet off of the ground.

I laid in my bed, shaking and shivering. Because I knew where it was going. To the big bay window in my room. Eight more feet to the right. And there it was grinning, smiling and gnashing it's teeth. I think the meat was just an appetizer for this thing. I could barely breathe. My wife and kids were upstairs. I was afraid to call the Police for fear of they would think I was insane. My gun only held five rounds, a really stupid New York State Law. I would like to turn this Beast lose in a crowded legislative chamber and see how fast the gun laws got changed.

It's form reminded of the werewolf creature in the film "Underworld.". This thing appeared three feet up in my window and is hunched over. That means if the window is three feet off of the ground, he is over seven feet tall. I was only relieved my house was made of stone and brick. The windows were the only weak access point. At that time I realized there was a foul smell emanating from outside. A combination of blood, urine and rotting meat. The smell reminded me of the smell of chum on a fishing boat.

It's taunting went on for minutes as he checked window after window. I was thinking a thirty round magazine and a bigger caliber would be better if legal. I think the heads up optics and laser sight on my gun would work well, they always had. But the five rounds of nine millimeter just would not be enough for this beast I would just anger it. So, I stood down and waited.

Minutes went by, as it paced back and forth from window to window. Growling and snarling, marking it's territory. My security cameras did a poor job catching it on video. It seemed to avoid just the right places. Eventually, it decided to just walk away on two feet, casually like a person.

My family HS decided I watch too much horror television. They didn't realize what I saw was real. The scratches, the smell, all indicated it was not a dream. They just did not understand why I was so scared to be alone. But I would lie here waiting for my visitor as prepared as I could be. I felt like the boy who cried wolf!

Chapter 3

More of the Blackburn Beast

So, if the definition of insanity is doing the same thing and expecting a different outcome…

trying something different is probably a sign of intelligence.

It began that night a few hours after moonrise. The full moon seemed larger then normal perhaps, brighter too. I had been asleep for a few hours. My room was the family room, off the back of the house. It was part of a single story extension attached to the kitchen. The roof was about eight feet off of the ground at the low end and twelve feet off the ground at the high end. There was a skylight in the kitchen and two in my room. They were operated by a switch on the wall to open and close them.

As it was hot that night, I had turned on my ceiling fan and opened my skylight about a foot. I am not sure what woke me up, was it the loud sound, or the smell of rot that filled my nostrils. I thought something was on the roof. No, not a squirrel or raccoon. Something much larger. It was over the kitchen twelve feet away. I heard it walking on the slate roof, loud heavy bipedal foot steps.

I realized I was such a fool. The beast was back and it found a way in. As I was in bed for the night it would take five minutes to put on my legs to turn off the fan, close the skylight or get a gun.

If it got to my skylight the only thing stopping it was a screen, that was if it can fit thru the skylight opening. The growls snd snarls were typical, the fear and nausea took over my body.

I feel I was just waiting for the inevitable. It must have jumped onto the lower roof. I was glad there are no windows into the upstairs from that roof save two small ones maybe a foot high and two feet wide. Probably, not big enough for the beast to get in.

The moon is high and right above me, I could see the silhouette of the beast over the skylight. I figure it would rip open the skylight and just drop in on me. I watch horrified, as it's arm and claw come into view under the open skylight just above the screen. It is playing a game of cat and mouse. It's claws slowly pierce the screen. I hear it's breathing and snarls clearly. It was only ten feet above me. I reach for my phone, I gave the side button five quick clicks. That transmitted my location, medical condition and an SOS for help to the police. At that point a padded room seemed safer then my home. I sat and waited for the cavalry to arrive. It appeared it could not fit through the skylight.

They turned out pretty fast, I think the sirens and flashing lights scared away the visitor. The officer who arrived before the ambulance saw the skylight and the screen. The officer closed the skylight. Once, the paramedics had come in he and another officer pulled their weapons and went into the back yard. Flashlights and pistols out they begun their search. Other then some dirt on the roof and evidence of two huge footprints side by side fifteen feet from the house, there was nothing. They figured who ever was on the roof lept off and landed there. Very large feet, not human more like a dog's paw print. They put down a dollar bill for scale and took pictures. They said they would look into it.

As for me, my blood pressure and pulse were way too high, so I spent the night in the hospital for observation. At least I would feel safe in the hospital with limited access and much higher roofs.

The battle with the beast would have to continue. Just like in the movie "Highlander" there. Can be only one! I just hope that it turned out to be me.

Chapter 4

The Beast of Blackburn Strikes Again

I was an observer by nature. I think it came from being a bartender and looking for trouble. Years of looking for the problem child who walked into the bar. But many times I never saw him coming.

So as I had said, when I moved in twenty two years ago my yards were covered with rabbits. Hopping around eating my flowers and grass, I didn't mind as I love rabbits. But they seemed to be all gone, I just don't see them anymore.

The garbage cans had been an issue. Over the years I had tried ammonia, bleach, new cans, a garage to hold the cans and nothing worked. The animals always got into the trash. So my family stacked garbage in the car garage. They took it out Tuesday, Thursday, Saturday in the morning just in time for the garbage truck.

The landscaper, complained that the neighbor's dogs had dug up the front lawn he worked so hard on. I had mentioned, that I had not seen any dogs as of late. But since there were burn marks on the back yard I figured a dog had marked his territory. All of these things were just background noise.

It was unusually warm the night of the full moon in April. Called the pink moon, for what reason? I don't know. That time after midnight, the night was different. It started as a distant bay. It grew louder. I had heard a cat screamed, then a dog barked then stop very abruptly. All the while,a haunting baying. The beast had returned and was coming closer.

I heard branches snap, twigs crack and then I heard what sounding like a dog playing push-pull with its master. That was what drew me to the window. In the backyard, I saw the bane of my existence, the beast. With a crushed cat in one claw and a large dog in the other. It took turns burying it's face in each, it ripped the flesh from their bellies. It was like watching a shark feed. Ripping, tearing, shaking it's head side to side. It was terrible.

I've had it at this point. Instead of looking for the phone, I pushed my panic button on my wrist.

It's a medical alert bracelet, the operator responded in seconds. I reply in a low voice that there was an intruder in my backyard killing dogs and cats. I State, "I was in fear for my family's safety, and my property was posted".

It seems the response time was slower this time. The sounds from outside were mind numbing. The smell of copper, no blood filled the air. Time passed so slowly when you need help. It seemed to slow down.

By the time the cops showed up the damage was done. There piles of fully eaten half eaten pets about the backyard. A patrolman called in a multiple 10-45 (animal carcasses).

One spot reminded me of a eaten bowl of chicken wings after Monday night football. Just a pile of bones, no meat or skin. Because of the scene, the patrolman changed his call and adds code 10-78 (need assistance).

Just as he does, he spotted something moving in the bushes. His light and pistol had come up instinct-fully. The cop wetted himself as the seven foot beast leapt towards him howling. After all, the beast had marked this yard as his. Shots rang out, I was a shooter I'm guessing fourteen maybe fifteen rounds. A full magazine of nine millimeter no…it sounded like a Glock forty.

Smoke and howling could be heard as the beast took off through the trees just as probably fifteen patrol cars pulled up. How the patrolman survived, I do not know. The bullets did not do much. A scant few rounds found their way to their target. I thought back to when I almost used five measly rounds on it.

The police fanned out and called low flying helicopters and dogs. It was like a scene from "The Fugitive" but real not a movie. The hunt for the beast went on all night. Statements were given, reports were made, it was a long night. The coroner shows up to get the animal bodies. When I asked about their autopsy he corrected me to tell me, "with animals it is called a necropsy." I tell him "dead is dead, does it really matter?" It was then I realized he just hated me.

My yard really looked like a war zone. At that point I started to think, dead spots in backyard, dug up front yard, the missing rabbits and the garbage cans, all point that he had marked his territory and was defending it.

I could only hope that they would hunt it down and kill it very soon.

Chapter 5

The Chase of the Beast

After the animal mutilation and shooting on Blackburn Lane the beast had fled. After all it was wounded. It headed west, towards town. Under the full moon, utilizing backyards, it stayed off the roads and avoided street lights. Pets hid in their master's homes as it neared. As there were no fences allowed in the village of Munsey Park, it traversed from property to property with ease. Just west of me was a small public park with a pond, we called it Pollywog pond. It stopped instinctively to drink water then changed direction to a more north west direction.

Between the police cars, the K-9 units and the County Police helicopter and their infrared cameras, they were trying to track it. It moved across the village effortlessly. Sometimes on two legs, sometimes on four. It then crossed over to the adjacent village of Flower Hill. There too, it was unrestricted. They forbade all fences in the front yards, and backyard fences were limited to a four foot height.

Utilizing properties and wooded areas it made its way. They eventually followed it to the Long Island Railroad train tracks. There were no lights, no police, no cars, it picked up speed, it was on a perfect trail. It crossed a main road while on the tracks, it headed north now. It crossed yet another village line into Plandome. It was picking up the pace and only the helicopter could track it.

Located, south of the Willowdale bridge in Port. Washington, but east of the train tracks lay a man made stream. A series of stepped catch basins and waterfalls used to control street runoff. It followed the path of the train tracks. It culminated at a large reservoir. At the end of the reservoir, there was a twenty foot waterfall.

This was where the beast had decided to go. It washed itself in the waterfall. A bit further north, the county dog pound, a few hundred feet away from the pound, there was a supermarket and it's dumpster. Lastly, a quarter mile north was the towns graveyard. Basically, a buffet.

The beast seemed to not need food, as his pet meal seemed to be sufficient. It changed direction and followed the water. That took him onto Plandome Golf course. A few more backyards and it was in Plandome and Leed's Pond. It followed the water's edge to Leed's Pond Preserve. A vast refuge with no people. It disappeared into the woods.

Somewhere, in the preserve, the pond, the golf course or the reservoir this thing found it's home. My backyard was just one of it's feeding grounds.

The Police had been great, but had not really helped to avert my fears. I had always noticed a patrol car parked at the entrance to Leed's pond. I just wondered why they choose that location to park?

Chapter 6

Preparing for The Beast

This tale found me still alive but living in fear. As stated before, I had three security systems. Wired and wireless. Infrared, glass sensors, shock sensors and cameras. I had decided to put up a fence within the permitted area for the dogs. I did not expect it to keep out anything.

As a child of ten, in my closet behind my clothes I mounted all my guns. Cap guns, disc guns, water guns etcetera on the wall. Just like a spy. It is the same now with my real guns, except by law I have to keep them locked up in gun safes. Guess politicians have never been robbed or needed to defend themselves. So I decide to break out a few, just in case.

After the situation in the backyard with the beast and the police, I had decided to up my game. So for defense, I thought about my favorite Marlin lever action forty five. Fourteen rounds without breaking the law. But decided perhaps not, but I would keep it out. My JRC 9millimeter was cool and all, laser sights, heads up optics, I can't miss but caliber is too small. So. I decide to pass.

Mossberg 500 pump with five rounds. I could alternate double ought buck and Slug. Buck, slug, buck, slug, buck. Yeah, I would consider it. My HK SL6 five rounds in two twenty three, I think no, too much risk down range, Lastly, I reached for another favorite. My Marlin 45-70 government. Aka my Buffalo gun. Deadly crushing stopping power. Drop a Buffalo or Rhino at one thousand yards deadly to three thousand five hundred yards. Yeah I know, what if you missed. It would probably go through a few houses. But, what if I did not miss. I could have ended it, that night if it showed, after all, this gun could stop a truck.

The moon was not full for another day, I thought. I choose two…the 12 gauge, and my Buffalo gun. Shotgun for close quarters, Buffalo gun for anything over fifty feet. All the rest were stored and locked. I grabbed five boxes of ammo from my ammo locker and put it in my room. The last touch was I strapped on my US Navy Kabar knife as backup. I debated putting on my body armor, not for bullets but for preventing claws from ripping me open. I would think about it was too heavy.

Geared up, I practiced clearing the house. Room by room, slicing the pie as is taught. Doorways, hallways and open rooms, a tactic to look around corners. It was a good thing my family had moved out.

It was just me, alone, in the dark. Waiting, simply waiting for the beast to return.

Chapter 7

The Beast Recovers

So, a few weeks had passed since the beast was shot in my backyard. It had laid low. Nursing itself back to health. Somewhere in the Leed's Pond Preserve. No roads, and no people but plenty of good food. It does not go out in daylight but prefers the cloak of darkness.

Bunnies, squirrels, fox and geese all available. It tried for a heron on the beach but failed, the eagles were too big and too formative. It would go to the pond first and search then the golf course. A few ducks sense him coming and start murmuring. He misses his dinner. It follows the pond shoreline towards the golf course. It is there on their pond he grabs a goose.

Although, the dining room was full with dinner guests, dancing and drinking, no one noticed that on the eighteenth hole, the beast evicserates the goose. No one cared. It devoured the goose as it walked, casting what was left into the green side bunker. The beast decided to head towards his favorite feeding ground, the cemetery. Thing about a cemetery, there are no cameras and little security. It had learned the fresh piles of dirt are what it wants. Having located one he digs.

After some time he finds it, he can smell it, fresh meat. This coffin is sealed but with a pull it opens. It grabs the lifeless soul and retreated to cover to feast it does not like feeding in the open.

Fully satiated, it jumps on the train tracks. The one eleven am train from Port Washington came down the tracks, the beast jumped off the tracks before it was hit. The Engineer thought he saw something but would not swear to it. The beast got on the tracks and followed the train almost matching its speed.

It spends time off the tracks in Plandome near Rockwood then Flower Hill Near Dogwood Lane.

Again thru backyards and front yards it traveled unrestricted. It has healed, It walked effortlessly. It now seeked water and it found it's way to Pollywog again. It waded in the small pond and drank water like a human , cupping it's claws to hold the water. After a few minutes it's thirst was satiated for now.

As it traveled through the rhododendrons and groomed properties, it hunted what it could find. It was killing not for hunger, it killed for the sport of it. It's first human victim was smoking a cigar walking his dog. He was dead before he hit the ground, his throat had been slit. As he lied dead in the street, his little yap yap dog was licking the blood off the street. No one heard or saw anything, there were really no street lights in the village.

It was close to three in the morning when I heard the typical rustling of trees and bushes as it came through my property line. I don't really sleep and I was focused on survival. What went thru my mind was a debate. Do I shoot first thru the glass and window frame or wait for it to break the glass. This certainly would drive me crazy.

Dumb as it was, I decided to wait. I had chosen the shotgun for close range. Problem with shotguns close quarters is they are really messy. Damages everything. I was however, locked and loaded. Unbeknownst to me, the County cops had been surveilling me. Basically using me as bait. Like a goat staked out for a t-rex, I was exposed. They had about a dozen BSO (Bureau Special Operations) in the area. Night vision, automatic weapons grenades they were ready. This would prove to be a disaster. I thought of what Ronald Regan said," I am here from the government and I am here to help!" I saw the headline in my head, "Beast killed , homeowner killed by friendly fire,"should have left with family.

Well, some rookie tried to confront the beast. What ensued was basically a firefight. To be clear, I did not fire as the rookie was in the field of fire. It did not prevent the hut hut guys from opening up. HK 93's I think. No telling how many rounds. The only thing they are missing was a mini gun. The icing on the cake was the two helo's they have circling at six hundred feet. No doubt filming their mistakes.

What I know, was there were a lot of dead trees after that and a couple houses that needed some serious repair. So much for training. Pray and spray is what they did.

True to form following its instincts, it escaped to the backyards and headed back to the preserve. The police tried to follow, but they were used to humans on streets, not animals in the woods. No officers were killed but a few caught a few friendly fire rounds in the arms and legs due to crossfire. The bricks on my house now have divots from where the rounds hit, amazingly none of my windows were hit. Props to the cops for not killing me or themselves. The good news I was still alive, bad news was the full moon was actually tomorrow!

Chapter 8

Following the Beast into the Woods

Over time, we had learned that it does not come out during the day. Furthermore, we learned it probably lived in the Leed's Pond Preserve. A rather densely forested area that was a non populated area near the golf course. The helicopters had narrowed it down to a postage stamp area. This was where the stupidity was really stepped up a few notches. The cops decided to send in a team to search and destroy. Here was the thing, they may dress like special forces and have equipment like special forces, but they are not actually special forces. This was not going to end well.

About twenty four men decked out in black and grey (great camouflage for the forest) fanned out and entered Leed's Pond Preserve at dusk. A perimeter had been set using available roads. This flaw in their thinking was what indicated incompetence. An animal does not care about road blocks or security and does not fear police presence. The police thought they were the hunters but in reality, they were the hunted.

As they search the forest it appeared to them there was nothing around. They were half right, what they did not realize was the sounds of the forest, birds, squirrels, insects raccoons were not present. The woods were silent. Had they been hunters and not cops they would have noticed it. They were told to look for a cave or den. They should have been told to keep their heads on a swivel.

When the beast attacked the first man, the beast dropped on the unsuspecting cop from a twelve foot high branch. The cop let out a scream, that is until the beast tore out his throat. The next two to die was a Lieutenant and another patrolman. Upon seeing the beast at a distance the lieutenant said," we are going to need a bigger boat!" The patrolman was pondering that statement as the beast killed the lieutenant. I don't know whose screams were worse, the patrolman's or the Lieutenant's. As the Lieutenants abdomen was slashed open by the beast. The beast then turned on the patrolman and feasted on his neck and face.

Their screams echoed through the forest. As their screams died off, the beast started his howl. Lower at first, then higher. It was more of a victory scream then anything else. After all he was defending his territory, and this let everyone know who was in charge of the forest. These few deaths had been happenstance for the beast. It then ran to the perimeter, it started killing each and everyone. Killing and circling the forest the screams echoed through the night air.

In the center of the Forest, the few survivors took up a defensive position. The last thing they probably heard was the helicopter radioing in the beast's position, one hundred feet and closing. Ultimately, it would not make a difference. The first two had their arms ripped off, their arterial blood shot eight feet in the air,they were both dead in two minutes.

The next two were not so lucky. All their guts spilled out on the ground as the beast tore open their midsections. Truely a painful death. They writhed in pain as the beast decided to continue on them or or not. It chose to let them die slowly. The last two could hear the men groaning in agony that before the beast killed the first by tearing his throat. The last and final policeman was killed when the beast swung at his head and knocked it clean off. The police man stood there for about a minute, his body not realizing the head was detached. It rolled across the forest floor like a fumbled football. With that the beast was done.

The helicopter pilot realized the police were all gone based on their radio silence. He called into headquarters to relay the problem. He was devastated as twenty four of his friends and colleagues were gone. This bought back the nausea which he was tough, but it was inevitable, he vomited. Headquarters decided to call the military for help. It would be a few hours before the Navy Seals would be on scene. He almost closed his eyes to pray, but thought better if it. So he prayed with his eyes open while flying, that the Seals would be successful. He flew back in total silence as all the radios were now and forever silent.

Chapter 9

Tracking the Beast

He was an active kid, he was a body builder,motor cross rider and black belt in high school.

So, upon graduation he followed in his father's footsteps. He became a police officer. He joined the County Police Department and became proficient in all types of weapons. As luck would have it after a few years he elected to transfer to Los Angeles. Just in time for the Rodney King riots.

The crash course in policing.

He continued his training, taking special courses in weapons, he became a fixed wing pilot. He decided to go back to New York.

There he decided to send himself to Helicopter school. After becoming a chopper pilot he found himself in the aviation bureau of the County Police.

In his spare time he donated his time to a World WarTwo airplane museum and an armored museum, he drove tanks. He became an expert on military history and tactics.

At work he was assigned to a special task force. He was the senior officer in charge of tracking the beast. He had arrived at the heliport early that evening. They learned the beast only comes out at night.

"Sarge" as he was called, grew up near Leed's Pond. Actually his Dad was the policeman stationed at the entrance to the preserve. He remembered his father's words of wisdom as he took off. When responding to a call "never turn your back on the the subject the husband or the wife." In addition, "never get caught out late at night near Leed's Pond."

Kind of made sense considering those current circumstances and situation. Flight time to area was ten minutes, with about two hours of fuel.

He had an observer on board to work the forward looking infrared recorder, the other cameras and the powerful searchlight. They would use the FLIR that night. They arrived over the area and started their search at six hundred feet, they circled the area in a quarter mile radius.

The night was deathly still at that hour. The only noise was the sound of the helicopter rotors, the three villages were use to the sound as the helicopters have been out for six months searching at night on full moon nights like that one. They searched, the preserve, Leed's Pond, the golf course, the woods and yards in between. As they hovered over the last village they had come across a man down. He was on a street near Polliwog pond. He laid in what looked like a pool of blood, there was a small dog on and around the man's body.

A click of a microphone and Police and EMS were called to the scene. Police to secure it, and EMS to aid. They don't know the man had been dead for quite some time. They continued their sweep, no one was out. No exercisers, no dog walkers just the downed man. People were taking heed of the curfew imposed locally. Until that night, it had just been animals and cadavers, now it wanted warm live people.

From his vantage point, he could see the hut huts (BSO teams) as they tactically searched the surrounding houses close to the pond. They cops used night vision glasses the pilot and observer used infrared. Like in the movie "Predator 2" the one with Danny Glover in the meat packing district. The infrared picks up heat signatures. Hoped this went better than in did in that movie.

This search had been unproductive, the pilot ran low on fuel in the chopper. Hopefully, his backup will pick up where he left off. He headed back to base frustrated he could not help, disconnected because he was six hundred feet in the air above the action. But tomorrow was another night, after he landed he got into his Audi A5 and raced home. After a good nights rest, he would be ready to fly again and track the beast.

Chapter 10

The Police up their game on the Beast

So, after the night when 24 men lost their lives, the Chief of Police picked up the phone and dialed for help. The first call went to the FEDS, FBI specifically. Being well aware of the situation they choose not to participate. The Chief's second call was to the Navy. The Navy under JSOG (joint Special Operations Command) put a call into Newport News, Virginia.

Orders were faxed over. In the military it is the only form of truly secure communication. Telephone, radio and satellite can be hacked, but not fax. Within two hours a seal team platoon of sixteen now called DevGru (Development Group) boarded an Osprey for a one hour flight to Republic on Long Island. It was a tight knit team lead by two seasoned Lieutenants one named Rip. He introduced himself to the two newbies in his team. When he stated his full name of Lt. Rip Taylor, one newbie was about to laugh when a Sargent stopped him saying" if you want to live, don't say what you're thinking.

The young seal stifled the laugh.

The other lieutenant was an animal named Lt. EJ Hartman , the men said his nickname was the "Terminator" for many reasons. Size and looks mostly.

It was a quick one hour flight, the Lieutenants described the deployment and situation. It was sImple, set up a civilian perimeter, two hundred and fifty feet inside a secondary perimeter wired with flares, M18A1(Claymores), Concertina wire (razor wire).

Coordinates are handed out maps exchanged electronically coms are up both Seal phone sat cons and the two-way blue tooth they use on the teams. They landed and deplaned and loaded on a two and a half ton truck. It would be an hour to the Preserve and an hour to hump in and set up. Each Lt lead a squad in the platoon. Classified by weapons, the Lt.'s along with three men per squad carried an m4a, two squad members carried the SAW MK-48 (squad automatic weapon) the M4a was NATO 5.56 and the MK-48 are chambered in Nato 7.62. Finally, two squad members have the M203 40mm grenade launcher. Lieutenant EJ thinks the only thing missing is a mini gun. Rip reminds him, "hey Rip, no terminator shit!" He means cutting down the forest with the guns. E.J, smiles snd chuckled to himself. The squads slip into the forest.

Unlike the police who seemed to be like fish out of water in the forest the Seals were right at home in the woods. They searched and found a location to set up a fatal funnel, a location for a crossfire ambush. After setting ip positions, they unpacked blood and meat to draw the beast in. As the beast started to smell the blood he moved towards the trap. At the very last minute the Lieutenants got the call to switch from deadly force to non lethal.

Rip is beside himself, but he knows these orders come from way up in the chain of command. He knows they wanted it alive to capture and study it, to weaponize it. They would use the same gas fentanyl, that was used in the Russian Movie theatre. Terrorist attack. That was where seventeen died from that non lethal gas. Hopefully it would work.

As the beast enters the funnel instead of shooting it with bullets, they used gas grenades by hand and the M203's. Within

Sixty seconds the beast was down and out. They humped the beast out to a large field at the preserve. It is a great lawn by the museum itself. They shackled and chained the beast. It was also caged as the Osprey came in and landed one hundred feet away.

They were now on their way to a top secret location. We knew it as Plum Island. In reality it is a covert maximum security prison that the government keeps things like cryptids and mutants in. Just like the prison for mutants in the comic "X Men." Thirty minute flight after capturing the beast, they drop it off at Plum Island. EJ turns to the men and says "and now it's Miller time!" They grab a few from the prisons fridge and hoped back on the Osprey for a quick flight home. No injuries, bad guy caught, all in all, a good day.

Chapter 11

The Beast in Captivity

Off the coast of Southold Long Island, in Gardiner's Bay sits a small island. Discovered in 1604, Plum Island got it's name from the wild beach plums on its shores as well as the pink sand on its's beaches, when wet at high tide it turned purple.

Purchased in 1899 by the US government. It was later designated the Plum Island Animal Disease Center in 1954, studying contagious animal diseases. But this is just the story they tell you. In actuality, it was a Super Maximum security prison for the most deadly creatures and humans in the world. It is the Gitmo of the weird and unusual. In 2008, one of their captives escaped and washed up on a Montauk beach, it was known as the Montauk monster.

The Seal team, after landing rolled the cage into the sally port of the prison. The director took one look at the sleeping beast. He immediately points them to the "Fox Mulder" wing. That was the highest security for the most unusual captives. The beast gets a shock collar and an ankle bracelet for tracking puposes.He is chained to the wall inside his cell. It will be fed twice daily a diet of red meat, blood and produce via a slot under the door in a bowl. A long stick is used to push and remove the bowl, there are no humans allowed in the cell. It sleeps on bed of leaves and straw.

Overtime, there had been many things learned about it's habits.

It lived predominantly in Leed's Pond Preserve. It hunted at Leed's Pond, Plandome Golf Course, and the backyards of Plandome,Flower Hill and Munsey Park. It preferred nightly activity, it avoided street lights. Cats and dogs ran away from the beast it knew no fear. It preferred it's food fresh and warm, mostly meat. Sometimes it killed for food and other times for sport. It probably could swim long distances. At first it would not eat in captivity, until a guard heated but did not cook the meat and blood. At that point the beast gorged itself. Lastly, it grew more hungry near the full moon.

It escaped from the facility by breaking it's chains snd removing it's tracker. Someone had left a door open after cleaning its cell. After killing three guards, it left a pile of mutilated prison guards, he killed for sport that time not food. Once in the hall it was easy, thanks to the fire exit one way doors. Once in the open it followed its senses. Following the moon and running in a southwest direction it covered the one mike width of the island in no time. It found itself at Plum Point where it dove into the water without hesitation. The water was cold, not sure if it was more current or swimming, but it ended up on Gardiner's Island near Botswick Point. It followed the eastern shoreline, it passed the lookout tower, Tobacoolot Pond and Great Pond. Halfway to Cartwright Island, it dove into the water again. It swam south south east, just by looking and following the moon. It finally landed near Hither Hills State Park.

For two days at night the beast followed the shore. Off season there was no one around. It ran the beach. By sound view beach by the bars, a customer thought they saw something but by the time someone checked there was nothing there. At Grossman's dock it choose to swim the inlet to Gin Beach. Heading east on Gin beach it ran a quarter mile. Seeing the tallest point it ran and crawled to the top of a hill to an abandoned look out tower, just east of the lake. After resting it travelled a few hundred feet into one of the many parks in Montauk. Unspoiled areas with ponds, deer and no population. Unlike its normal habitat, it found this seaside environment suitable, perhaps it has found a new home.

Chapter 12

The Hunting Grounds

So from just east of the airport in Montauk past the big Reed Pond east to Shagwong beach. To the south passed the Oyster Pond to the east to Montauk State Park to the south Camp Hero and finally to the west the Sleepy Hollow cattle ranch. There was plenty of food.

It had come across the three seals on Shagwong Beach. It killed two of the three in the forty degree water. The deer it usually found bedded down at night in the tall grass by Reed or Oyster Pond. It killed a deer by each pond. It lived a carefree life hunting and killing, unchallenged. That isn't to say it did not have problems. It did stray too close to the airport and the light house on different occasions. One time while looking at seals from the bluff at Camp Hero it almost fell off of the cliff. Lastly while hunting cattle at Derp Hollow it killed a horse instead. For that the rancher took three shots that missed.

Until the horse, it had lived on deer and seals. The horse killing brought it attention. Luckily for all, it was early spring. Tourists had not arrived as of yet, town and beaches were still quiet. That however would probably change. Afterall, an alpha predator with no known weaknesses would be a problem. Specifically, if it just started killing for fun. The beast did not understand but instinctively knew the blue creatures would return as well as the black and grey ones, inflecting more pain. The beast grew angrier and angrier thinking about it if he only knew how to think or what anger was. Right now he was just running on animal instincts.

The first human sighting of the beast was a Wall Street stock broker. He was driving to the Montauk Light. As he drive at dusk a herd of deer ran along the south side of the Montauk highway, they paved him at thirty miles an hour. At the last minute one jumped over the guardrail and slammed into the car. It destroyed the passenger door, front quarter panel and the windshield.

The driver stopped the car about one hundred feet passed the impact. As he backed up the distance, another creature jumped over the rail and bent over the carcass. Illuminated by only his reverse lights he decided to turn around. When he got close enough his headlights were bright enough, he could not believe what he saw. A werewolf like creature feasting on the dying animal. Tearing and eating it with its mouth and claws. The Wall Street guy's only thought was to take off heading back to town really fast. He hit the gas in his BMW 733 and rocketed past this thing to get back to town. He decided that night he would never vacation in Montauk or go out east again. For him the furthest he would go is Brooklyn or maybe Queens.

Chapter 13

The Best Place To Feed

When the beast gets hungry in March, April the early part of spring It looks for a colony of seals on land. So, Shagwong Beach, Turtle Cove or Seal Beach would be it's choices. Second choice would be the same locations but in the water. In the water they are called a raft not a colony.

Deer are a totally different animal. The beast hunts them too in spring when the yearlings are born and the mothers are tired from birth. The lay down in the tall grass by the ponds a herd of five or six. By the Oyster Reed Ponds. It will even venture near a roadway at night for road kill, deer killed by cars.

Lastly, it developed a taste for cows and an occasional horse. So going to Sleepy Hollow Ranch, for the Beast was like going to a great steak house for us. The beast kills, eviscerates his prey ate some and carried the rest off, basically a doggie bag. He would take it back to his lair and eat it for days. From time to time it would forage in a restaurant dumpster, it does not like that usually too many people, too much noise and too many flood lights.

He hydrated himself with the blood from his kills it gave him nutrients. It drank water that it got from the ponds, pretty much nightly. It drank a lot and the temperature is not even hot yet. At night it is in the thirty's, yet it's metabolism is so high it needed the calories, so it had to feed.

It slept during the day, and hunted at night. Whether on the beach, in the surf or on the grass it was simply a killing machine. On a spree with no end in sight. With no one, nor anything to challenge it as of yet, this would probably go on for awhile.

Chapter 14

Food Supply Starts to Wain

As the seasons changed, so did the beast's food supply. By April, the seals which use to cover the beaches, had left. The deer had learned to avoid the beast as best as they could. There weren't too many cows on the ranch to begin with, the ranches mostly had horses. The ranchers definitely had an opinion about the beast killing their trail horses. They liked to dissuade the beast with bullets. So the beast found himself more hungry than usual searching for food.

There had been many sightings of the beast by May in Montauk. It was no longer a myth or a scary story told by firelight late night on a beach. With the rise of spring temperatures the beast found new food sources humans and tourists!

The first was a local who spent too much time in the watering holes in Montauk. That particular evening the beast was close to town and came across a restaurant dumpster. The beast, smelling food climbed into the dumpster. As bad luck would have it, a man staggered out the back door of the bar restaurant and started to relieve himself on the dumpster. The drunk was looking down while urinating and never saw the beast stand up towering over the dumpster and the man. The beast raised it's clawed hand and arm and nearly tore the man's head clean off. He was still urinating as the beast bit the few connective tissues that held the head to the neck.

That night, after feeding, the beast ran. Under the night in the darkness in the presence of the full moon, it ran. It loved the night and it loved killing. What the beast would never know is that by killing the patron at the restaurant the Police would now be involved. By morning, news of the murder had swept through the sleepy little fishing town. By noon, there were Police and local hunters out searching the parks for the beast. Resources were limited here, no high tech gadgets. Just the cops and few east end deer hunters and an occasional fisherman off his boat and out of season.

For know there was no rhyme or reason for their search, like a bunch of kids in elementary school at recess, they all went their own way. But, this chaos would not last long. The second murder of two young kids saw to that. They had ignored the curfew and found a remote beach that night. The boy's plan was to build a fire, drink some wine and maybe loose his virginity. It seemed the girl was more than willing, but halfway through the fire and their intimate act, the beast came upon them. The boy had been on top in the missionary position trying to catch his rhythm, when the beast attacked. The girl had been enjoying it slightly,but the last thing the girl felt was her lover's blood splattering on to her face and breasts, they both were gone instantly, victims of the beast.

What was left of their bodies was discovered the next day by an early morning jogger. The Police marked off the area. There were many civilian onlookers. Of course one of the fisherman looked and said," looks like two shark attack victims!" What the fisherman did not know was that he was pretty close.

It did not take the Police Chief of this small summer fishing town to realize he was in over his head. He had read the stories of the beast from the previous year. So, he picked up the phone and called the Nasssu County police for help and advice. They gave the Chief two numbers, The FBI and the NAVY. Nasssu's advice." Forget the FEDS just call the NAVY!" So that is exactly what he did. He was advised the special Seal team would be there on site in less then three hours. The Chief put down the phone, sat back in his chair and breathed a sigh of relief. He thought to himself at least now help is coming. At the time he should have realized just how bad this was going to get.

Chapter 15

A New Dawn

As the sun rose over a lonely beach in Montauk New York, the sunlight reveals a crime scene guarded by a lonely police officer who guarded the scene surrounded by crime scene tape. The horrible murder of two teenagers had the town buzzing. The patrolman took a sip of his coffee and tried not to look at the gruesome scene. He thought to himself, it's going to be hard not to get sick, seeing and smelling the remains, he swallowed twice, once for the coffee and another time yo keep what's trying to come up his throat, down.

Mean while, calls have been made and plans put into motion

After their early morning training,Lt. Rip and his squad of Navy Seals fall into the mess for their chow, it is o'seven hundred. They are temporarily stationed at Little Creek just outside of Virginia Beach Virginia. They were Seal team three normally out of Coronado California, They specialized n mini- sub sea infiltrations usually behind enemy lines. They were in Virginia for advanced training. As a team they had done everything together, breakfast was no different. They all had lined up, grabbed there eggs, hash browns toast and sausage, grabbed a coffee, water and sat all at one table. Eating off these metal trays was better then field prepared rations. It was kind of tight but the team of seven plus their leader made it work. After all these men had been in tighter situations then what the had there that day.

Somewhere, between the eggs and hash browns the Lt .'s beeper went off, followed by the beeper on every Seal at the table. The first message said "Report Active Duty". These beepers were used by the brass to notify them to report for duty. The next text message read "Critical Mission Priority: Alpha". In unison without words, the eight man stood up, grabbed their trays dumped them in the garbage and left in silence. They were used to this. All the other enlisted men in the mess were not. The muttering of where they were going or what they were going to do started to spread. The mess buzzed with rumors. Everyone wanted to know the scuttle but that day.

The team hightailed it back to pick up their equipment and gear. They were on the tarmac within the half hour. They rendezvoused with Lt. EJ and his team. Rip, After getting his orders, simply relayed to the men. "The Beast, Montauk, New York, Search and Destroy." The men knew their jobs, they had been trained and had the skills. They did not tarry in rendering their equipment operational. Rip relayed further info, "Destination, West Hampton Beach Air National Guard Station. They would get ground transport from there."

They called their Osprey, the "Seahawk" and it made great time to their destination. It covered the distance at three hundred and fifty knots per hour, or about an hour and fifteen flight time. Upon landing they commandeered three humvees and a truck from the Air National Guard Station. They loaded their gear and headed east. It was a one hour drive from West Hampton to Montauk. The roads were relatively clear as it was now late spring early summer, traffic during the day was not too bad. Besides, everybody moved out of the way for the giant green armored convoy.

Rip had taken a radio call on the airplane ride up. The brass was sending a Hawkeye E-2c to cover the area and requested the National Guard. The Hawkeye was known as the eye in the sky. Rip felt.he needed something more. The Hawkeye was great at mapping ships and planes but they were tracking a land based animal. So over the mic to command he made one request "REAPER!" Rip knew the M-Q9 REAPER was the best hunter killer attack drone the US military had. With an air speed of three hundred knots and a range of eleven hundred miles. Controlled by ground station Nellis outside Las Vegas, it took off from it's base in southern New Jersey was one of the only ones on the east coast. It was on station, on guard and hunting by the time Rip and his team landed. This was modern day warfare after all.

As the team rode down Montauk Highway heading east,they looked at the expensive homes. Well, the first town of Hampton bays, maybe not so much. But by Southampton their minds were changed. Beautiful million dollar homes. As the towns clicked by, Watermill, BridgeHampton, East Hampton and Amagansett, it was all the same. More money then you could dream of. Behind them, about an hour away, a convoy of National Guardsmen were rolling down the highway. Approximately one hundred twenty four guards were in five trucks. Their MOS (Military Occupation Specialty) were all different. But all were needed.they consisted of:

Infantry (Field 11)

Construction and Engineering (Field 12)

Field Artillery (Field 13)

Military Police (Field 31)

Civil Affairs (Field 38)

Public Affairs (Field 46)

Medical CMF (Field 68)

Transportation (Field 88)

Mechanical Maintenance (Field 91)

Quartermaster Corps (Field 92)

These would all be necessary to lock down the town of Montauk.

By the time the Seals had hit the town of Montauk. Their opinions changed. It was a small summer fishing town at the end of Long Island. Except for the large beach houses worth millions, they were hard pressed to see expensive houses. They continued eastward thru town heading east on Montauk Highway towards the Montauk Lighthouse. The area out here was pretty desolate. Once the got to the State Park they pulled off on a northern road into the forest, there they found a clearing. This would be their jumping off point and later their rally point. It was not even noon by the time their boots had hit the ground. Rip thought to himself, "this would be a very long day!" With the Reaper circling above hunting, they pitched camp. The plan was to set a perimeter, lined with trip wires, claymores and flares. When it was done. With that completed, Rip thought he could breathe a little easier knowing he and his men were a little more safe.

During lunch, the coms popped up. The National Guard had simultaneously set up two lines of containment. One from Napeaque Bay on the north due south to the Ocean. It was a few hundred yards wide. Wire, lights, flares, claymores and armed soldiers. It had a hard checkpoint on Montauk Highway, no one in or out. The next one was at the eastern perimeter of the town. It ran from on Fort Pond Bay , from the Captain's Quarters restaurant on the beach due South following Edgemere along Fort Pond, thru the circle to the beach and ending between the hotels. The Coast Guard supplied two twenty eight foot boats and a forty one foot boat along with five twenty five foot inflatables for inshore shallows, bay and lake searches.

Rip, thought to himself, "with the perimeters set, waterways covered, camp set, chow downed it was time to get to work. From each seven man squad he pulled two men. One M4A, and one MK-48(Saw)and placed them on perimeter watch. He would lead the other five as would Lt. EJ into the forest on recon this afternoon. They had about seven hours of light left at this time of year, and he planned to use it. Tracking tracks, placing trail cams and launching a small drone. Unlike the Reaper this one was unarmed. The RQ-11 Raven only captured videos and stills. He found it very useful and he had used it in Afghanistan.

Chapter 16

The Recon

Perimeter set, food downed, time to make the donuts. The team headed out looking for a larger clearing to launch the Raven a small Unmanned aerial vehicle(UAV). As they went on the game trails they saw signs of game and unusual scat. They put up two of their twelve infrared trail cameras used for night surveillance. Motion activated, blue toothed and cellularly connected they would provide great Intel on what was out here at either day or night. There plan for day one and two was map the area, nightly searches would not start for a few days.

They spent hours on recon, had noted topography, terrain, flora, fauna in hopes of tracking the Beast. The moon rose over the east end as the sun set in the west. This was Rip's signal to return to base. He put one man on point and they all headed back to the bivwak area. They radioed in on approach to the perimeter, after all, they would not have wanted to get shot. Although tired, they rotated guard duty after eating their chow.

The nights menu was of course MRE but a fine choice of Beef Stroganoff or Chili, having had Chili Mac for lunch, most chose the Stroganoff. It was quite dark on the east end at night. The stars were amazing as there was little light pollution. They banged into each other at times, as they chose not to use flashlights, lanterns and no fire as these would be dead giveaways to their location.

Occasionally, red head lamps were used but only by some. As they reviewed there first photos they were pleased. They caught good images in daylight and at night. By twenty one hundred hours(9pm) they were dark, all men had gone to their two man tents. These four season tents did the trick. As far as sleeping bags they all used a snugpak system. Two mummy sleeping bags numbered one and two. They would use only the number one as it was good to forty degrees. If they had inserted the number two into the number one, it would be good to zero degrees. As it was close to forty at night, the number one would suffice.

The men thought of course of the Beast, but soon they pretty much thought of home. Their wives, their children or girlfriends. Some were married, mostly the older ones. A lot of the young ones had not been hitched. Those men had not even any thought about it. Payday, drinking, new cars and chicks that is what they thought of. I can't fault them for that kind of thinking considering their ages. By twenty three hundred (11pm) they all were asleep , except the perimeter guards. They would swap out later that night. All men would get their much needed rest. In a few days the true hunt for the Beast would begin. Tomorrow, would be another grueling day.

Chapter 17

The Seals Settle in

Camp was pitched, perimeter set and know they broke out their chow. MRE's or meals ready to eat. Most men grabbed the go to, "Chili Mac." Each man made his own. Good but a hard cry from the mess hall chow. They sat and ate and took in the views of the forest. They noticed it was mostly coastal oaks, being red and black. Holly, flowering dogwoods, redbuds and plums would round out the foliage.

Lt. Rip, took a moment and looked at the newbies. He had been like them. He had come a long way from his start in the teams. His first paycheck being a mere seventeen thousand dollars twelve years ago. He could not believe he made about three hundred and fifty thousand dollars a year now. He deserved every penny for leading that team into battle time and time again, against all enemies. They were usually foreign, however this time it was domestic.

There was something about Seal training. All the training becomes so ingrained that it becomes automatic in behavior.

The camping, the cooking, the equipment repair, the weapons, the endurance, the searching. It would all ties together and was almost effortless. Then of course you had the Seals. They had become one, a band of brothers. They know the man next to them had their back and would have given his own life to save their life. Adding up the points, makes them one of the most formidable fighting forces on the planet. That is why they could always hold their heads high.

Chapter 18

The First Overnight

The overnight had been uneventful. At checkpoint Alpha and Bravo the two National Guard perimeters were fine. Except for the irate civilians who wanted to enter or leave town. This had been an issue. They had learned that the Beast was not what most people thought it was. It was not a man who changed into a werewolf at night. It was just a weird type of animal. It was always a werewolf. So the main concern was security not contagion.

The first rule of security in a combat situation, secure your borders. Those that complied at both checkpoints went home. Those that did not were arrested and jailed in an old super market closed for renovation. It had been completely empty but then was filled with people. There had been about one hundred people detained who had tried to get in or out of the secure areas. They would have plenty of time to think about their mistakes, but for now they were safe.

Back in the Seal camp, at o'five thirty (5:30am), every man was up. Most ate MRE oatmeal, while some had picked eggs but all opted for coffee. It was not like a venti Starbucks, but it would do. Any thing that would start the body up in the morning was good. These guys ran on adrenaline, caffeine, food and water, in that order. It was every Seal's job to get his fair share of each.

After the quick breakfast, the men prepped for day two of reconnaissance. Same as the day before, but twice as long and two to three times the distance. They lightly covered yesterday's search area but rather focused on the outlying areas. The pulled their gear and went out on patrol. About two hours into the search, the Coast Guard reported in. Overnight they had added to the boats on scene from Coast Guard Station Montauk. A forty one footer out of Coast Guard Station Shinnecock. It came by way of the Atlantic ocean. The other two boats were twenty eight footers from Coast Guard Station Shinnecock located on the Peconic Bay and traversed the Peconic River to be on scene. Rip filed that information into the back of his mind and acknowledged, he pressed the men on further with the reconnaissance.

In an open field they quickly launched the Raven. The eight man seal team was down to six including himself because of perimeter watch at base camp. Normally they would put up a sniper in over watch but that needed a spotter for security. That would leave the team down to three plus the Lt. So, he decided for the safety of the team, he kept the team together. He knew they were best as a unit. They put out their remaining trail cameras. They covered the trails and strategic points on or near the beaches. All feeds were up and running trail cameras and both drones.

The reaper was pushing infra red as well as 4k digital videos. The best thing about the Reaper was it was armed with two Hellfire missiles, to be used if the situation warranted it.

At thirteen hundred hours(1:00pm) they break for lunch. It was random choice meal, each man chose something he wanted so it varied. Lt. Rip decided it was time to up his game. He called in for air support. His call was answered by ANG West Hampton with three Sikorsky HH-60 Pave Hawks.

They would be launched and on scene in one half hour. Fighter with night vision , search light and two automatic door guns they were a big asset to have had available. They could circle the entire area in about thirty minutes, day or night with a two hour flight time. They would request a refueling truck be placed a Montauk airport. This would keep their down time limited. Their only disadvantage was the rotor noise. But Rip welcomed their addition.

Montauk is humming. From the checkpoints, to the street patrols to the coastal searches, the helicopters and the dronc's over flights, this is modern day warfare all day and all night.

This town "Was" on lockdown.

For the Seals, more area patrolled all afternoon. They ate chow, they reviewed camera footages, the sentries were relived. All in all a good day, no one wounded, no one dead.

Lights out as usual. Rip said a quick prayer for his men's safety and a quick , peaceful outcome that gets them home safe and sound.

Chapter 19

The Hunt begins

The day had started early in the Seal's camp. Everyone was up, excited to start. They would do the usual MRE, coffee combo for breakfast. They had finished up and started working on servicing their equipment and weapons.

A few minutes later Rip got a radio transmission from the Alpha gate. Overnight, the Martinecock Indians had shown up fifty strong. The elders had said the Wolf summoned them. The Wolf was a symbol of loyalty, strong family ties, good communication, education, understanding and intelligence.

However, when they got close to the gate the sensed it turn evil. It was not a Wolf that had summoned them. It was a Windigo, an evil shape shifter.

So they had set up camp to pray and burn sage. They built a special lean-to hut, next to Alpha gate. They were embedded for the duration.

After that call, Rio told the men about his plan. He would send four men to town and search out two large trucks. Then they were to go to Gossman's dock and the wholesale warehouse. They would liberate all the inshore herring they could transport. That was the fish the seals eat in the shallows.

Within the hour two trucks arrived in camp full of fish. The plan to dump three foot high piles of fish throughout the forrest near game trails with cameras. Building different rings of placed fish. closer towards the middle. Each truck drove into the Hinting aground. It took the men a few hours to get the job done. In the center of the rings they had caught and killed a large buck for the main course. The men had been hungry so the washed up and MRE'd again. They were working up a sweat. Rip decided to take them back to camp. They would grab a quick bit of rest and relaxation, after all tonight was going to be a very long night.

Chapter 20

Preparing For Night Moves

Both teams had regrouped back at the camp. The seals had downed their chow and rested for four hours. They all grabbed some shut eye in their respective bivies. Lt. Rip , appeared startled as the coms started blasting intense chatter. Having grabbed a radio it sounded like the National Guard was under attack. He called for sit-rep from all stations A sit-rep is the current military situation in a particular area. Coast Guard checked in all clear, as did Alpha checkpoint and Bravo checkpoint, the only non responsive unit was the one guarding the make shift prison.

The mic was keyed occasionally, yelling and screaming had been heard over the airways. He ordered the perimeter points to stand their posts. His team would respond. His estimated time to target was ten minutes or less. He ordered the helicopters in stand-by for an overflight asap. He and both squads saddled up and high tailed it back towards town. As he went he regretted his thought of keeping one hundred defenseless people in an empty supermarket with a Beast on the lose.

As they raced down the highway westwards towards town, Rip radioed checkpoint Bravo to move the barrier as they approached. They blew through it at over forty miles per hour. As they pulled up to the supermarket in the middle of town, he noticed the guards were dead.

The team responded, six surrounded the building, two secured the vehicles, each Lieutenant led three men into each door. One team took the front door, one team took the back. Rip led the front assault team.

The carnage they discovered was as bad as they had seen in Afghanistan. Piles of bodies, mostly dead. Blood, flesh, urine, and feces. The sight and smells made a few sick. Just as Rip, the leader of the front door team came around the end of what was the produce aisle, he was attacked. Claws ripping his flesh, tearing his muscles to the bone. He heard teeth gnashing, he thought no one had fired! He collapsed and laid there dying in agony.

It was at this point, he woke up screaming, back in camp. As his men rushed to him. He started to get his wits about him. It had been a nightmare. Holy crap, where did that come from. He had never done that before. He always operated under a high stress environment. He planned on talking this out over a few beers, after the mission. For now, he just strapped on his boots and guns, dismissed the men from his tent, and stepped outside. He noticed it was just about sunset. He muttered to his men, "Come on, we're are burning daylight!" He stopped himself to clear his head and simply breathe.

it was now about two zero hundred(8:00pm), the team, after that was ready to rock and roll. Tonight they would be in over watch. Drones, trail cameras, night vision, mostly visuals on the piles of fish and nearby trails. They hoped to capture sightings and new trails of the Beast. The men split up into their teams. One perimeter team, two Recon assault teams. As they left camp, they all noticed the sun had set for the evening.

Chapter 21

Night Moves

Lt. Rip, was still shaken from his

dream. His discomfort was added to by the use of night vision goggles. He used them for years, but he never really liked them, The team got to their drone launch clearing quickly. After launching the Raven they split up, one team north west. The other team north east. The last comment Lt. EJ spit out was," Good Hunting Boys!". Both teams moved silently into the darkness.

The Beast had been up for awhile. It roamed the forest seeking food. The natural wildlife had learned to avoid areas the Beast claimed.

In this vast series of natural parks and raw land, it did take the Beast sometime to find the first fish pile. It circled the first pile and waited. After ten minutes it moved in. Sniffing the air looking for problems. Finally it took a few fish. These Herring could grow to sixteen inches in length snd weigh about two point four pounds. The Beast decided to just jump on the pile as it was easier to eat that way.

After fifteen minutes of eating the Beast got off the pile, he then stepped back snd urinated near but not on the fish. Turned out by marking his territory no other creatures dared to venture near it's food.

The process was repeated for most of the night. It was caught on cameras more then with visuals. What alarmed the men was the speed at which the Beast moved and the distance it had covered in very little time. The men realized they could not chase it, as it ran at better then thirty miles an hour. They would have to ambush it. Catch it unaware.

By nights end they had filmed and somewhat studied the Beast. Even with their high tech equipment, they eventually lost sight of it. It would take time for them to locate and kill the Beast.

As dawn approached they headed back towards camp, Lt. Rip had a thought came into his head, so grabbed a radio. He quickly radioed the National Guard and ordered them to double the guards at the make shift prison. As he put down the radio, he sighed a sigh of relief and thought "not on my watch.!" They all hit the camp as dawn broke over the eastern horizon.

Chapter 22

Everyone Makes Bad Decisions

Matt, was a young man, he was a fisherman and a surfer. He had grown up in Montauk mostly his whole life. After all, his father owned the house on top of Prospect Hill. Which sat on the east side of Lake Montauk, the Italian style mansion and grounds had the highest elevation on the east end in Montauk. It was about noon, It was daytime so he invited a few surfer friends over for a day of drinking. It was lonely on the hill top as it was secluded and it was not quite season. He drove around alone in his old surfer's car, a yellow Jeep Wrangler with soft top, doors and gathered his friends.

They arrived back at the house and started drinking just the four of them as no one else was home. They felt safe there as the property was fenced and gated. The home itself was built of stone and concrete block.

Matt was pounding down cocktails like a professional. The others, Trip, Suzy and Brittany were no slouches. Hours of drinking and listening to music, this crew felt no pain.

As night time approached they all started thinking about food. The house had a professional kitchen. One of Matt's brothers was a professional chef so the house was stocked very well. They prepared filets and sides then Matt went down to the basement to the wine cellar and just flat out raided it. Grabbing a few of the best red wines he could, his Mouton Rothchilds find, he took his pillaged bottles upstairs. He was careful with the close to four thousand dollars he held in his arms. Their meal was ready, so they sat for about a two hour meal.

Having finished dinner, they mutually decided to further break curfew. The girls wanted to go to the Montauk Light, even though they knew it was closed.

So they played a quick game of rock- paper- scissors and decided their fate. Brittany would be the driver. They went out to the yellow Jeep and loaded up and got in. Upon starting it she intentionally did not turn on the headlights. After all it was now about nine thirty and it was a curfew during lockdown. There was enough moonlight to drive, although she did so cautiously and carefully. No lights and driving drunk were not a good recipe. She drove towards the Lighthouse at about fifteen miles per hour. She turned on the radio.

About a mile away, the Beast was foraging for food. No longer enticed by the cold piles of fish, it hunted, using its senses it ran and searched. It's eyes, ears and nose were trying to pick up the sense of prey. It was his ears that picked up on something first. To the south and east it seemed. It quickened it's pace. When it got within five hundred feet it could smell something, multiple prey. It ran at better then thirty miles an hour, it closed the distance. Finally, at two hundred feet it could see them. It's eyes adapted to be able to hunt at night. It sensed more the creatures in the car than the car itself if it could, it would have said," Yesss, warm food!"

It came upon the Jeep, quickly.

It approached from the driver's side. It moved quickly and silently. It's claws tore thru the plastic driver's window like a hot knife through butter. It's five foot arm with claw, killed the driver and the passenger with one thrust. The jeep slowed to a stop, as the driver bled out. The blood and assault on the front seated passengers made the two in the back push themselves back towards the rear window. The Beast had followed the car from behind. Like a frustrated child tearing open a bag of chips, it dispatched the rear plastic window. It was then upon them.

Matt did try to shield himself by using Suzy as a shield, but it bought him three seconds of life and an eternity in hell. The Beast would take his time feasting. First, the kids in the back, then the kids in the front seats. It climbed out the back, being full it, relieved itself. It now left Montauk Highway and it entered Camp Hero to the south. It entered the familiar woods, it has been there before. It looks to the moon and howled. Searching forever searching.

Chapter 23

Overflights at Night

The Air National Guard helicopters swept the area from the first entry gate to the Montauk light. They flew staggered three abreast. Using night vision and infrared, they flew at six hundred feet. They had over lapping field of vision. The pilot and observer had Infra red and the door gunners had night vision which worked off of starlight, it made everything look light green.

Heading east, Chopper one flew and viewed the southern shore front, Chopper two flew and views just north of the shore front to just south of Montauk Highway. Chopper three flew and viewed just south of Montauk Highway and into the forest north of the Highway.

It was chopper three that picked up the stopped Jeep on the Highway.

Chopper three who found it stopped and hovered over the jeep. Chopper one and two circle d back and flanked chopper three on either side. Forming a line heading due south they slowly advanced over the Camp's forest. The pilot and observer of each helicopter checked the forest for the Beast. Night vision goggles were of little help as the canopy was too thick. So they relied on the infrared in the cockpit. As they advanced they radioed the ground forces searching the hunting ground.

Chapter 24

Meanwhile, That Night

The Seals had been searching the Hunting Grounds and forest to the north. They had waited near the fish piles and the game trails with not much luck. It wasn't until they heard the radio chatter from the helicopters did they realize the Beast was south of Montauk Highway. The two lieutenants decided to rally their teams to the last known position m, that of the disabled Jeep. They double timed it to just near the road. They huddled up roadside just north of the highway. The lieutenant then gave orders for them to fan out in a skirmish line and then gave the command to advance. They would see the helicopters a quarter mile ahead flying at six hundred feet. They advanced into the woods about eight feet apart towards the helicopters.

The helicopters found the Beast hard to track in the woods. But by using their night vision and infrared, they were able to catch glimpses of it under the canopy of the forest. The helicopters didn't get a good view until it was seen at the old radar dish building at the camp. By then the Seals had caught up and by using selective fire at the Beast, drove it further south towards the shore away from the radar dish.

Again, the Beast who had been here before ran much quicker than the Seals. The helicopters pursued it. Towards the shore it ran where the gigantic sized shore batteries once stood. During World War Two, there were many shore guns built on the east end. Looking like a battleship gun turret but fixed on shore. These were to deter submarines. Three sixteen inch Iowa class naval guns sat in each gun battery. The breach and crews had room to operate and live. Those guns had a sixteen inch diameter and could fire a shell twenty miles out to sea.

The Beast headed towards one that the blast doors had not been sealed closed properly. When the Beast got close to the doors, the gunships were hot on his trail, they got the order to fire. They opened up with the door guns, laying down a rain storm of bullets. But the Beast managed to enter the battery, through the open blast doors unscathed. As the choppers poured on the lead, the Seals took up an observation position. They radioed in the Predator. They authorized one shot at the door to seal it in and kill it. The Seals would have to aim a laser at the doors for the Reaper's missile to hone in on. The young Lieutenant, flying it back at Nellis Air Force base flew it like he was playing a video game. The Seal's did their job and the missile was inbound in thirty seconds.

Guided by the laser directly at the doors, though old, they did take the bulk of the blast. Although over eighty years old they were designed originally against aerial attack. What nobody knew, was age had left the door open, and on the sea side there was an exit. A small exit, none the less. One of the ports where the barrels had fit thru the seaside bulkhead had been sealed with concrete.

Over time it had cracked away and as of late, with young teenagers removing the remnants,had been removed entirely. It left an air hole beach side so the kids could get some air in their hangout. Just before the blast, the Beast used it as a fire exit. It climbed down the cliff effortlessly to the beach and headed west. The AIr National Guard and the Seals had been focusing on what they thought was the only way in or out. They waited for the fires from the explosion to die down to check for the body of the Beast, to confirm the kill. They were sickened, when they found no body and the giant hole looking out over the beach. The helicopters then widened their search but the beast was on the move and moving fast, west and north it deliberately tried to get home before the sunrise.

Chapter 25

Up in Arms

Next day sunrise came at five forty five AM. Everybody in town had heard about last night. They knew about the dead teenagers, and the explosion down at Camp Hero. They knew from the bagel store to the pancake house to the Super Seven convenience store, everybody was talking about last night's events. What was worse was everybody was getting angrier and angrier. The groups were mostly men but sprinkled within a few women. First it was small clicks, then it was small groups and large groups. Then came small mobs and then large mobs, these were all problematic.

Some groups took to the water to search the shores, some groups got in their four by fours and headed for the Hunting Grounds and forests. They all looked the same, both old and young men with hate in the eyes and guns in their hands. This was not going to end well. The National Guard and the Seals did much to dissuade many of the groups but there were a lot roaming free trying to catch the Beast, in the minds of the civilian's, they were going to kill it.

The groups that were fisherman although great on the water we're not good at hunting an animal that roamed on the land. The hunters who were hunting the Hunting Grounds and the forests, never realized they were in over their heads. After all they had never hunted an animal like this before. Shotguns, high-powered rifles, pistols, bows and arrows they had it all. There was even one guy dressed up in a medieval knight's suit of armor thinking at least he wouldn't be ripped apart or bitten. He had a hard time with his broadsword., however. Both the armor snd sword had been heirlooms from his family. And the National Guard and the Seals had no choice but to start locking up these various vigilante groups. The number of people being interred in the make shift prison in the supermarket was becoming astronomical. Head count was up to two hundred eighty three, so far. This all happened before 11 o'clock in the morning.

The Seals and the National Guard had all their hands full with the civilians. They all thought, if we can just get through until tonight. We will catch it. What they had to do was avoid killing a bunch of civilians before nightfall or watching the civilians kill each other. They realized the civies probably had no shot at killing the Beast.

Lt. Rip and his men, felt that the time set aside for breakfast and lunch was probably going to be the best part of the day. They also knew this would get worse before night fall.

Chapter 26

Good Old Boys

That afternoon the Coast Guard spent its day chasing the boaters who were hunting the Beast from close to shore. The National Guard focused on the perimeter gates as well as the wire fences in attempt to keep the civilians from border hopping. The military, whose job that afternoon was to keep the hunters out of the hunting ground in the forests was pushed to it's limits.

By 4 o'clock that afternoon, Lieutenant Rip had had enough. He told the air National Guard to fly low and suppress civilian activity. He told the national guard to increase the non-lethal force used against agitators. They had seen a rash of men using ladders to go over the wire. The Seals, after watching a bunch of good old boys jump there four by four over the perimeter fence, Rip, told his man to just put the spurs to them, so they did.

After controlling the civilians,

His teams went out on early patrol and searched out the hunters, stripped them of their guns and locked them up. The teams passed them over to the Guard. The Guard would transport them to the jail. The formula was simple. Catch, transfer snd repeat. By dusk they had cleared most. So they regrouped back at camp before moving out for the evening.

Lt. Rip, wanted to get this job done. Next plan was to radio Nellis. He got on his seal phone, which was a satcom radio set. Secure transmission was set immediately. Normally, the deck or the minimum altitude for aerial operations was angel's ten meaning ten thousand feet. Rip asked for a hard deck of five thousand. Only when the mission went "Mission Close" could it drop lower during and attack to one thousand. The immediate area was already designated a no-fly zone for all other non military aircraft. Loaded with two Hellfire missiles the Reaper would be primed and ready for action.

Meanwhile, the Air National Guard were operating at six hundred feet. Doing search grids with infrared. In a few moments,

The Air Guard keyed the mic. They had picked up a very large mob of hunters in the Hunting Grounds apparently in a skirmish line with burning torches. They were trying to flush the beast and drive it south towards Montauk Highway. The helicopters could see the Besdt at times just in front of the hunters.

As the hunters eventually crossed the highway. The Beast had doubled back and killed the two hunters on the west end. Quick kills they never saw it coming, they fired no shots it was so quick. The Beast did not feed. It was killing for fun snd survival. The attack caused the line to collapse inwards towards the middle as fear grew in the ranks. Right after that the teams caught up snd reinforced the line.

They all drive it further south. Until they could see it in the distance. It was near the radar dish building. There was an eight foot security fence surrounding the building. The Beast was almost the same height as the fence. The Beast, simply jumped over the fence.

The untrained Hunter fired the first round. Then the rest felt obligated to fire as well. The Seals held fire as the Beast climbed the exterior fire escape towards the roof.

This now was becoming a symphony. The helicopters circled with their flood lights.

The hunters had stifled their firing. The Seals stepped up and took shots at the Beast. The Beast deliberately avoided the edges of the roof. It stayed to center under the ancient rusted super structure of the radar dish. A Cold War remnant of an early warning system known as the dew line.

The scene was unreal, the Beast up on the roof top, and the angry townsfolk with torches yelling for death. This scene looked like a scene from a famous horror movie. They tried tear gas, direct line of sight shooting. Straggling runs from the gun ships. Rip decided it was time to unleash the Reaper.

The Beast was a "Clear and a present Danger "and The mission was designated "Danger Close". The wind was usually out of the south snd tonight was no different. The young Air Force pilot at Nellis Air Force Base, flew the Reaper in bound from the north and dropped to one thousand feet. He cleared the Air Guard from the air space. In bound as the Seals used their targeting lasers. The drone pilot worried snout his miss last time, he would not make that mistake again. About a mile out, he let two Hellfire missiles off of the chain a speed of close to one thousand miles per hour they followed the lasers on target in about sixteen and one half seconds. The explosions were twenty feet to either side of the Beast

The fireball was massive, engulfing the super structure of the dish. Either through melting or collapsing the super structure fell on to the roof top and the Beast. Eventually the ceiling collapsed and the building burned. The fire department did not respond, there was too much risk. So they just let the building burn all night. The Seals as well as the Air National Guard set up a perimeter to let nothing in or out. With nothing left to kill, the hunters left for home. Having used both missiles and being low on fuel, the Reaper was recalled to base. The Reaper was the first military asset to leave and go home. The others looked forward to leaving soon. The full moon was overhead perfectly that nite at midnight. Hopefully, the Beast was dead forever.

Chapter 27

The Clean Up

In the morning the fire department did go to the site.

They circled the radar building and did a" Surround and Drown"

Whereby using pumpers they shot a water curtain all over the building. If nothing else, then to just cool off the site.

After the Seals search the remains they uncovered what was left of the Beast"s body.

There was not much left.

So much fear, so much pain this Beast had caused. It was staggering, now the time to go home Had arrived. The Coast Guard was next to pull up stakes. Then the National Guard after deconstructing the perimeters and they completed the processing of the prisoners. They too left this once again sleepy little fishing town.

It was down to two groups, the Seals and the Indians. The Indians had been chanting and dancing for days. With the perimeter barriers gone, the Indians now had freedom of movement, and they used it. Praying over every inch of the town and town folk The smell of sage filled the air. No one complained, the smell of sage now was everywhere. The Indians believed it was their destiny to help protect this town and it's people from the evil of this Windigo and all evil spirits that may be near.

Lt. Rip called in for an evacuation of his teams. Unlike the police in Manhasset, the Seals were leaving with their teams intact. All present and accounted fore was a great thing to hear. As they loaded the Osprey, they were light a few tons of gear. The SeaHawk took flight from the landing zone,

Rip thought to himself, "Thank God,that his prayer to God, really did work!"

Finis